Building HEROES

By Annie Auerbach
Illustrated by S. I. International Illustrators

LITTLE SIMON
An imprint of Simon & Schuster Children's Publishing Division
New York   London   Toronto   Sydney
1230 Avenue of the Americas
New York, New York 10020

First Edition
2   4   6   8   10   9   7   5   3   1
ISBN 0-689-86857-X

At 6:45 Monday morning B. J. was already at the work site. He was meeting with Lisa Gabriel, the architect, to discuss the blueprints. The plan was to tear down an abandoned old building and replace it with a new after-school children's center.

"I'm concerned about the schedule," Lisa said. "We've been delayed a month already because of the weather. What if we don't finish in time?"

B. J. had been a construction manager for fifteen years and had met this type of challenge before. "We'll do our best!" he promised Lisa.

By 7:00 A.M. the heavy-equipment operators had arrived and began to work. B. J. liked to hire people he had worked with before because he knew they were reliable and would do a great job. "We're on a tight deadline, so work quickly, but safely," B. J. told them. "Now let's start tearing down that building."

Crunch! Rip!

The demolition machine tore into the old building. A skilled construction worker named Jack sat in the cab of the demolition machine. By operating a joystick he sent the excavator's gigantic arm into the building.

Once it had grabbed onto a chunk of the building, Jack then mechanically closed the "grabber," pulled back the arm, and then swung the cab around and dumped the contents.

Eventually this powerful machine would demolish the entire building!

Back by the office B. J. and another worker, Sarah, were watching Jack operate the demolition machine in the distance.

"Jack always like to make a mess, doesn't he?" joked B. J.

"Some things never change!" Sarah agreed with a laugh.

"Why don't you operate the loader and clear out some of the rubble?"
B. J. asked.

"Sure thing, boss," Sarah replied.

Sarah slipped a pair of hearing protectors over her ears and climbed into the cab of the front-end loader. Operating the controls, she scooped up the debris in the loader's bucket. She backed up, turned around, and headed toward a dump truck. Then up, up, up the bucket went and—*thump! thump! thump!*—the debris was unloaded. Sarah went back and forth, dumping more debris each time.

The following week B. J. called together all the workers for a meeting. "Everything's going well, but we've got to make up some time," he explained. "How would you all feel about putting in longer hours? If we don't, I'm not sure we'll finish this by September."

The workers exchanged looks. They knew why September was so important—their *own* kids were supposed to go to the after-school center! They all agreed to do whatever it would take to get the job done in time.

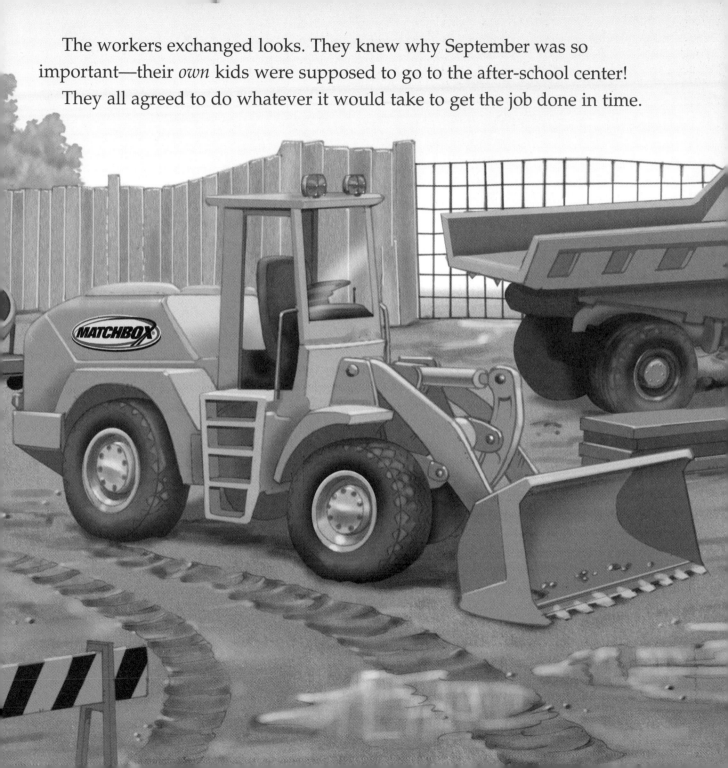

Everyone worked extremely hard. They would do long shifts, often trading off who worked nights and who worked days. Huge lights were assembled to help the night workers. Luckily since the building site was in a business district, no residents were affected by the lights or the noise. Although the hours were long, safety and quality were still top priorities. B. J. made certain of that.

By November the old building was gone, and the debris cleared. The new building would need a strong foundation of steel rods and concrete, so first a very large hole had to be dug in the ground. It was a perfect job for an excavator.

Once again Jack climbed into the cab and got to work. He used the controls so that the machine would scoop up a large load of dirt and gravel, swing around, and drop the contents into a dump truck nearby.

As soon as the dump truck was full of dirt and gravel, it was Tony's job to transport it to an off-site location. When he got there the back of the dump truck was tipped up and the contents were dumped out. Then it was back to the work site to fill up again!

Finally the huge hole was completely dug up, and Luis Alvarez and his cement mixer were called in. This vehicle had a special feature: To keep the cement from getting hard, it would constantly turn within the truck itself. Luis called it his "churn-and-turn machine."

Once the cement was sent from the truck on the conveyer, it was poured around steel rods. Together this would make the foundation safe.

Building the after-school center was strenuous work, but the machines helped the workers out tremendously. They could lift, dump, churn, and mechanically do things that saved a lot of time and strength.

But would it be enough to finish the after-school center in time?

As the months passed, Jack, Sarah, and Tony's jobs were finished. Now instead of heavy machines, smaller tools were used by a new group of workers:

welders,

electricians,

painters,

and landscapers.

The hard work paid off, and the day before school started, there was a grand opening and ribbon-cutting ceremony for the new center.

Everyone was proud of the construction workers—especially their own children.

B. J. thanked each of the workers individually. "I couldn't have done it without you," he told them.

And the workers couldn't have done it without the very large heroes: the construction vehicles!